W9-BUF-743

The
Rain
Stomper

For all girls who stomp
—A.K.B.

For Liz, the Rain Stomper
—E.V.

Marshall Cavendish Corporation, 99 White Plains Road, Tarrytown, NY 10591
www.marshallcavendish.us/kids

Library of Congress Cataloging-in-Publication Data
Boswell, Addie K.
The rain stomper / by Addie K. Boswell ; illustrated by Eric Velasquez.—
1st ed.
p. cm.
Summary: When it begins to rain and storm on the day of her big parade,
Jazmin stomps, shouts, and does all she can think of to drive the rain away.
ISBN 978-0-7614-5393-2
[1. Rain and rainfall—Fiction. 2. Parades—Fiction.] I. Velasquez, Eric,
ill. II. Title.
PZ7.B65125Rai 2008
[E]—dc22
2007013758

The illustrations are rendered in oil paint on Fabriano watercolor paper.
Editor: Robin Benjamin

Eric Velasquez would like to thank the children of the Sacred Heart School in NYC for all their help.

Printed in China
First edition
1 3 5 6 4 2

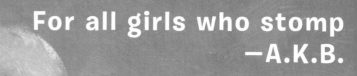

Marshall Cavendish
Children

The
Rain
Stomper

BY

ADDIE BOSWELL

ILLUSTRATED BY

ERIC VELASQUEZ

Marshall Cavendish Children

On the first day of spring,
Jazmin flipped out of bed.

She twirled her baton.
She swirled in her new red suit.
Today was the day of her big parade!
All the children on the block would join in:
Dancers! Drummers! Cheerleaders! Dogs!
Jazmin could already hear the neighbors
cheering and the

Tat-a-tat

Boom!

MARCH

2 3 4 5 6 7
9 10 11 12 13 14
16 17 18 19 20 21
23 24 25 26 27 28
30 31

Jazmin threw open her front door.

Wind whistled through her hair.

Thunder rumbled the ground.

The sun scuttled behind the clouds.

The sky twisted into a thick, black coil.

SLAP
clatter clatter
SLAP!

Rain poured down in buckets.

BOOM
walla BOOM
BOOM!

Thunder rattled the bricks in the walls.

clink clink

WHOOSH!

The wind plunged her family back into their beds.
Even the weeds slunk back into the earth.

Jazmin hated the rain.

It ruined parades.

It silenced the horns and the drums.

It tripped up the dancers and the dogs.

It soaked new red suits.

"Mud Puddler," Jazmin muttered.

TAP tippity TAP TAP

"Cloud Crasher," she complained.

CLACK clickity CLACK

"Parade Wrecker," she rumbled.

TAT rattle rattle TAT

BOOM

walla

BOOM BOOM

The rain roared.

BANG

walla

BANG

BANG

The rain crashed.

BAM

walla

BAM BASH

The rain bellowed.

BOOM

walla

BOOM,

walla walla

BOOM!

Jazmin stepped onto her stoop.
She lifted her baton
and shook it.

SLAP

clatter

clatter

SLAP!

Rain slapped against the sidewalk.

BOOM

walla

BOOM

Thunder rattled the windows.

BAM

walla **BAM**

BASH!

Jazmin shook her fists. She stomped her feet.

clatter

clatter

SLAP!

She kicked the rain down her steps.

splish

splish

WHACK!

She splashed it
down the sidewalk.

She chased the rain into the street.

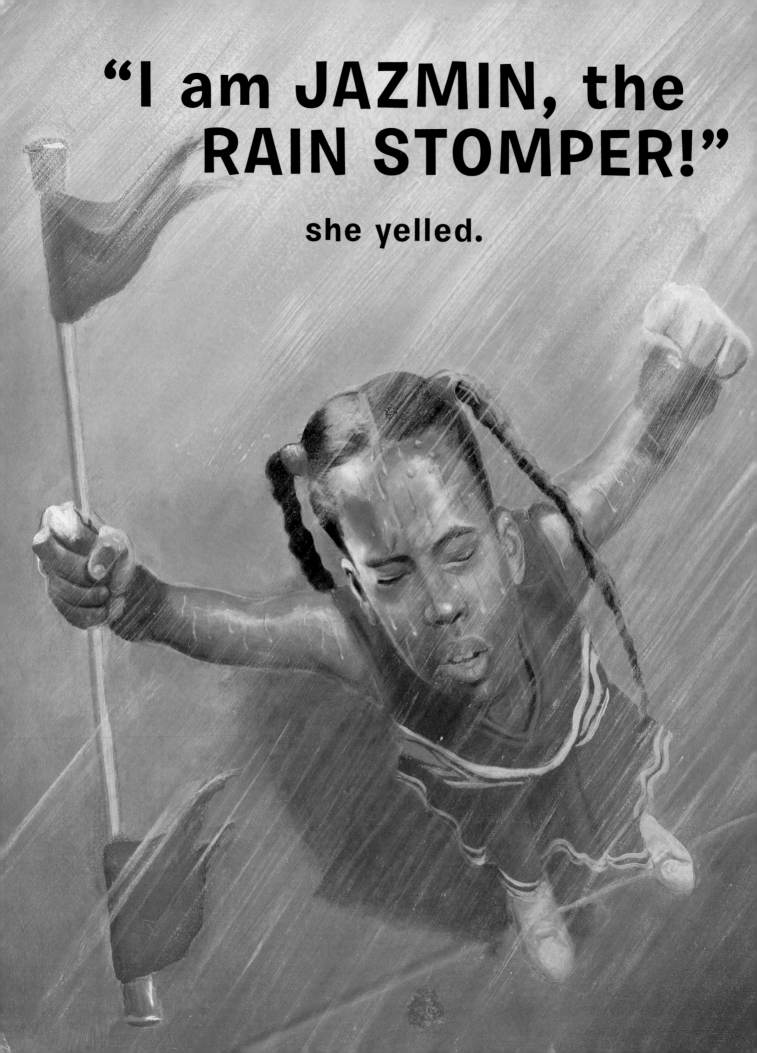

Jazmin **stomped**

and **splashed**

and **skipped**
and **shouted**
until . . .

children peered from their doorways.

"Splash some more, Rain Stomper!" they shouted.

"Splash higher, Rain Stomper!" they yelled.

"Stomp bigger, Jazmin!"

Jazmin splashed **more,**

and **higher,**

and **bigger.**

She **spun.**

She **shook.**

She even

*rat-
a-tap-
tapped.*

The sun peeked out and beamed.
The puddles shimmied.
The children cheered.

More children poured out of their houses.

They stomped and splashed

and skipped and shouted.

Then they
drummed
and **whirled**
and **flipped**
and **twirled.**

Children flooded the street.

(Even the weeds came out.)

And so it was that Jazmin, the Rain Stomper, and her parade of puddle splashers outstomped the rain.

SLAP
clatter
BAM
BASH!
BOOM
walla
BANG
CRASH!